I0604735

SCOURGE

Keith McArdle

Copyright © 2025 by Keith McArdle.

All rights reserved. No part of this book may be used or reproduced in any form whatsoever without written permission except in the case of brief quotations in critical articles or reviews.

This book is a work of fiction. Names, characters, businesses, organisations, places, events and incidents either are the product of the author's imagination or are used fictitiously. Any resemblance to actual persons, living or dead, events, or locales is entirely coincidental.

For more information contact :
(Email & Website)
https://www.razoredgebooks.com/

Edited by: A.J. Spedding of Phoenix Editing
Cover design by : Adrijus from Rocking Book Covers

ISBN - Paperback: 978-0-9925657-8-7

1779 - London

The room was silent, save for Rear Admiral James Roy's quill scratching the surface of the parchment. He stabbed a full stop and dipped the tip of the feather into a small pot of ink nearby. A knock at the door gave him pause, the quill bleeding black liquid onto the paper beneath it. He placed down the writing implement and swore under his breath. "Enter!"

A loud groan escaped the hinges as the heavy door swung wide to a candlelit corridor behind. Captain Blithely, the Royal Navy's most recently promoted officer strode through. His brows were furrowed, blue eyes piercing and mouth downturned, lips tight.

"Not good news then?" rumbled Roy.

"I am afraid not, sir."

Blithely unfurled a parchment and passed it across the polished wooden table. The rear admiral placed it flat on the table, one elbow on the wooden surface, hand supporting his chin as his eyes darted across the scrawled words. A heavy sigh passed through his clenched teeth, and he slammed down his fist, narrowly missing the ink pot. "Damn!"

"I quite agree, sir. Seven villages on the eastern seaboard—"

"Razed in the last five days," Roy finished. "*Seven!*"

"The pirate raids grow in

number by the month. How do we stop them?"

Roy continued to read, pausing intermittently to mutter. Finally, he leaned back in his chair and placed the parchment to one side. "We stop them using irregular tactics to beat them at their own game and destroy them one by one until none survive. That, my good man, is how we stop them."

Blithely's eyebrows almost touched his hairline. "Sir, we are bound by the law of *war*!"

"We fight these pirates *under* the law of war!" He gestured at the parchment. "And that is how it is paying off!"

"What do you suggest, sir?"

A smile stretched his lips wide, but the good humour did not reach his eyes. "We use Captain Ash against them."

A sharp intake of breath told him what Blithely thought of that idea. The younger man's mouth dropped open, and he remained silent for a moment. "Sir! We cannot use this," he gestured in the air, "this *monster* in combat. He will bring the Royal Navy into disrepute! I cannot think why he has not already been court-martialled and hanged!"

"If you want to fight pirates, my good man," Roy said, lifting the quill and dipping the nib in the ink pot before he looked up at the junior officer, "then you use a pirate of your own."

"A *pirate* is a good description of the man!"

"I agree he used some rather... non-conventional tactics against the slave traders. But how many slave ships did he stop?"

Blithely sighed. "Ten, twenty." He waved a hand at the wall. "I don't know."

"Forty-eight!" Roy continued scribbling on the parchment. "Forty-eight ships."

Silence reigned in the room once more, aside from the scribbling quill. Roy stopped writing and glanced up. "Is there any reason you are still here, Captain Blithely?"

"No, sir, I just—"

Roy pointed at the door. "Then you are dismissed." He continued writing. "And send Captain Ash in against the pirates!"

Blithely departed, closing the door quietly behind him. Rear Admiral James Roy placed the quill into the ink pot and leaned back in his chair once more. "Let us stop these bastards once and for all."

1779 – Somewhere at sea off the English coast

Captain Ash stared through his telescope, the distant beachhead brought suddenly into sharp focus. The rowing boat had been dragged up onto the sand and hidden amongst a copse of palms. Standing amongst trees of varying sizes and shapes were the two Royal Marines he'd ordered there no less than one half hour earlier. One held his musket across his body, muzzle pointing diagonally at the sky. The other had his weapon slung on his back, staring through his own telescope at something on the far side of the island. He then raised an arm high above his head with three fingers displayed.

Ash let the telescope drop by his side. "Three minutes!" he shouted. "XO!"

Lieutenant Basby, a rugged-looking man whose face was marred with scars, collapsed his own telescope and placed it away in a leather pouch. "Sir?"

"Raise the inverted colours!"

The XO turned on a heel and

started roaring commands.

While the mainland lay hidden on the far side of the island, the thick blot of black smoke drifting high in the sky from where a medium-sized British town was burning on the mainland, was not.

Ash glared at the swathe of blue-uniformed Royal Marines standing in rank and file upon the deck. "Marines! Load! No rounds, powder only!"

The captain looked beyond the Marines at his warrant officer, who stood beside a large pile of wood, a blazing brand in one gloved hand. Ash nodded, and the warrant officer turned to the pile and thrust the red-hot iron into the depths. He'd ensured the blaze was built at the opposite end of the ship to the magazine. Should the powder in the magazine ignite beneath their boots, the entire ship would be blown to smithereens in a white-hot explosion.

Captain Ash glanced over his shoulder. The Navy colours flew high, the inverted flag waving and snapping in the wind. He brought the telescope back to his eye and scanned the beachhead until his two Marines came back into focus. Two fingers were held high. Ash dropped the telescope to his side.

"Weigh the anchor!"

"Aye, sir, weigh anchor!"

Ash turned to the helmsman. "Hard to port!"

"Hard to port, aye!"

Captain Ash looked to the ship's bow. The anchor crew were

heaving the anchor winch, working well as a team. A deep *thud* that reverberated through the massive ship suggested the anchor had left the ocean's bottom.

"Forward sail down one quarter! Mid-sail down half! Aft sail raised full!"

Captain Ash raked his eyes over the ship's deck, watching each team of sailors working on their appointed tasks. He suppressed a cough as wood smoke permeated his nostrils. His warrant officer still stood by the smoky blaze, but a wet handkerchief was held over his nose and mouth. Sailors nearby stood at the ready with buckets of water in case the blaze threatened to spread to the ship itself.

The mighty HMS *Victory*, free

from her binding to the sea floor, started turning to port and, with gentle ease, slowly accelerated. Ash cleared his throat and raised the telescope to his eye again, searching for the two distant Marines. One index finger was being held high. Captain Ash collapsed the telescope and placed it away in a leather pouch at his hip before fastening it closed with a small leather strap.

"Marine command!"

Lieutenant Marks turned on a heel to face him.

"Prepare your Marines to fire."

"Aye, sir!" Marks turned back to the ranks of Marines. "Marines! Front rank, thirty paces for*ward*, march!" The front rank separated from the rest and then, after the designated thirty paces, came to a halt, their right boots slamming onto the deck. "Front rank *about*, turn! Front rank and second rank, pre*sent!*"

Marines pulled musket buttstocks into their shoulders and leaned forward, grim eyes staring down barrels. Ash tapped the helmsman's arm. "Forward," he muttered.

"Aye, sir." The helmsman turned the wheel back to its central position, and the ship slowly straightened. With sails at half-mast or stowed, the battleship would never reach her full speed, but she still cut the water with efficient speed. Ash looked back at the beachhead. The two distant blots sprinted for their rowboat, their duty complete. Beyond his distant Marines, movement caught his eye. It seemed the tips of the pirate ship's masts glided through the trees, visible one moment, hidden behind a mighty oak tree the next. She was moving fast. Ash's eyebrows drew together, lending his eyes a glint of anger. *That's ramming speed at the very least.*

Then the bow of the pirate vessel broke clear of the island's concealment, and the rest of the ship came into view as the prow cut through the waves. Within moments, the whole ship was clear of the island, her sails bloated with wind. She was huge and quick.

"Fifty guns at least, sir," said the XO.

Ash nodded. "Or more." He turned on his heel. "Marine command!"

"Sir?"

"Wait for my command, I want the bastards to see us before we waste good powder."

"Aye, sir."

Captain Ash clasped his hands behind his back and strode to the edge of his ship, stopping only when the handrail dug into his belly. He glared at the enemy vessel, willing for them to take the bait. *Come on, turn you mongrel dogs!*

Only when the bow of the pirate ship turned to put them on a parallel angle to the British battleship did a slight smile tug at the corners of Ash's mouth. "That's more like it!"

Ash shouted, "Marine command, have at it!"

"Fire!"

Muskets blasted to life, gun smoke blotting the Marines from view. "Reload! Powder only!"

The pirates were approaching fast, the ship cutting the water like a hot knife through butter. Ash hoped he had convinced them his ship was under mutiny. As far as the pirates could see, the warship had a fire burning on its top deck, sailors were firing upon one another, the colours were inverted, and the sails a mess. He wanted the enemy to believe the British ship was a plump, easy target to attack and raid.

Ash unclasped his hands from

behind his back and raised one arm above his head. "All ahead full!"

"All ahead full, aye!" the XO confirmed and roared commands.

The forward, mid, and aft sails were dropped simultaneously to their full length, and an audible snap resounded as the fabric filled with wind. HMS *Victory* surged ahead, rapidly accelerating through the ocean. Within a minute, they were outpacing the pirate ship. Another volley of musket shots rang out over the deck. Ash watched the distance between himself and his adversary grow and waited. His next move needed to be timed to perfection. Too late, and the enemy would lose its appetite for the chase and give up. Too soon, and the pirate ship would cut the British warship in half. *That's good enough.*

"Starboard anchor turn!" he shouted.

The helmsman spun the wheel hard right while the team near the prow released the heavy anchor, the chain roaring as it slid with blistering speed into the depths below. The anchor thudded onto the seafloor, and the chain went taught. A heavy, wooden groan reverberated through the ship as she rapidly turned to starboard and decelerated to a halt, now facing broadside and in the path of the oncoming pirate ship.

"Weigh the anchor!"

"Aye, weigh anchor!"

The team started heaving.

"Gun command!"

"Aye, sir!" drifted the voice of the officer standing near the manhole in the deck leading down to the gun teams beneath Ash's feet.

"Fire starboard chain shot!"

"Chain shot, aye!"

Muffled yells beneath Ash's feet suggested the command had been passed on. There was a clatter of wood on wood as the gunport lids on the starboard side were hastily thrown open and fastened in place. A moment later, a staccato of explosions vibrated through the ship, closely followed by the powerful, rhythmic whir of chain shots somersaulting through the air towards their target. The first chain shot embedded into the prow of the enemy ship, the second passed clean through a mast, and then the rest of the shot arrived in a swarm. Several smashed into the forward mast, cutting the mighty length of timber about ten feet above the deck.

Ash cupped his hands around his mouth. "Ready the port guns! Normal cannon shot!"

The gun commander raised a thumb at him and shouted down the manhole. Muffled yells erupted beneath Ash's feet once more. The gunners were skilled. Firing on a moving target was difficult in itself. A ship travelling toward the gunners meant they had only the prow and the width of the ship at which to aim. A much more difficult thing to hit than if they had been firing at the pirate's broadside. The forward mast of the adversary ship tilted slightly to the left, and then the fall of the heavy piece of timber accelerated. It slammed into the ship's gunwale, bounced slightly and then came to rest, part of the sail dragging in the ocean.

Captain Ash almost lost his balance as HMS *Victory* lurched beneath his feet. The anchor team worked hard and fast to pull the mighty piece of steel free of the sea floor.

"Full to port!"

The helmsman spun the wheel all the way left, and the British warship turned and accelerated, albeit with lethargy. Ash watched his opponent. They were approaching fast and turned towards him. He smiled. *They intend to ram us.* It was exactly what he wanted. Before the ship turned enough to be running parallel with the adversary, Ash tapped the shoulder of the helmsman. "All ahead."

HMS *Victory* accelerated almost to full speed, cutting the water with precision. The damaged pirate ship was slower but still aiming toward him. This presented their starboard side in an enfilade, still more difficult to hit than a true broadside, but he had faith in his gunners.

"Fire!"

A slight pause, and then all hell erupted beneath Ash's feet, the black dots of cannon balls scything through the air. One of them bounced off the ocean's surface, went airborne, slammed into the sea and disappeared within a water geyser. Gunners were trained to aim low to punch holes in a ship's hull beneath the waterline. *That one was far too bloody low!* Ash watched the fall of shot. Many of the cannon shots splattered onto the surface of the water at high speed, mere feet from the side of the ship, no doubt hammering holes through the wood, allowing gouts of water to pour into the depths of the vessel.

Ash slapped a hand onto the shoulder of the helmsman. "Full to port!" Then he cupped his hands around his mouth. "Port side guns reload grapeshot!"

"Grapeshot, aye!" came the distant shout that confirmed

Captain Ash's wish.

HMS *Victory* conducted a slow, wide turn, sailing back towards the pirate ship. But heading into the wind dropped their speed rapidly while their adversary continued to aim at Ash's vessel.

"Marine command!"

"Sir?"

"Prepare to board!"

"Aye, sir!"

Lieutenant Marks's shouts of commands faded into the background as Ash focused on the oncoming pirate ship. He clenched his teeth, his hands still firmly clasped behind his back. He leaned into the helmsman and offered a few quiet commands to ensure that when the enemy's ram hit them, it would only be a glancing blow. Movement in the corner of his vision made him look up. Several Marines were climbing high in the rigging and shuffling out along the masts' booms. Each Marine carried a slung Nock Gun, a seven-barrelled volley gun that rained down rounds upon the deck of the enemy ship. When they were in position, the Marines unslung their weapons and waited.

The Royal Navy ship, aided by the wind, was gliding backwards. On came the pirate vessel, cutting the water much faster than Ash's warship. They were moments from colliding.

"Brace yourselves!" Ash roared, grabbing hold of a rail and widening his stance.

The helmsman turned the wheel hard to port so that with their slow, backward drift, the front of the Royal Navy ship turned to starboard. The pirate vessel filled Ash's vision. A deep, reverberating *THUD* shuddered through Ash's body as the pirate ship slammed into their front port edge and then slid down their left side. The shriek of wood grinding against wood was louder than he expected. Pirates lined the side of their ship, swords, cutlasses and spears waving above their heads, their yells distant but growing louder by the moment. Ash homed in on one pirate – a giant towering in the middle of the throng, a musket pulled into his shoulder, but the man held his fire. The closer they moved, the bigger the man became. His dark-brown beard could not hide the sneer, and piercing dark eyes locked to Ash.

Ash waited until the giant was standing directly opposite as the two ships passed one another. He lifted his arm and dropped it towards the deck. "Fire!"

The cannons spoke with thundering voices, sending grapeshot at almost point-blank range into pirates milling at the edge of their ship. The grapeshot punched through soft flesh and shattered bone. One pirate's face disappeared in an explosion of blood and skull fragments, his body dropping like a ragdoll to bend double on the handrail and then topple over the edge into the thin body of ocean separating the two ships.

But the giant had not moved. Nor had he been hit. Then he disappeared behind a cloud of gunpowder. The sound of the musket shot cut through the raucous of screaming, groaning, and dying men. A loud buzz filled Ash's ears and then a sharp sting cut into the left side of his face.

He swore under his breath and wiped a hand down his cheek. His fingers came away bloodied. Ignoring the pain, he clasped his hands behind his back again and focused upon the Marines clustered near the gunwale, preparing to board the enemy's ship. Some of the pirates aimed up at the sails and fired, but their aim was as poor as the quality of their muskets. The Marines nestled in the rigging, Nock guns pulled in their shoulders, remained unharmed.

"Send the grapples!"

"Aye, grappling hooks!" roared the XO.

The bright steel hooks flashed in sunlight, their arc of flight slow and graceful. Reaching their apex, the grapples plummeted towards the pirate ship, slamming onto the deck. One of the hooks battered a man's head, blood exploding from his face. He fell screaming, cutlass clattering to the deck as he grabbed his shattered. The grappling throwers pulled the ropes taut with rapid precision, the hooks sliding across the deck until they caught firm on the gunwale, sunk into corpses, or gripped onto the gaps in the decking boards.

A deafening roar shattered the air, and the pirate ship disappeared in a mist of gun smoke. They'd fired a cannon volley directly into the side of the HMS *Victory*. There were muffled screams from beneath Ash's feet, where wounded Navy gunners lay bleeding, no doubt.

"Give the pirate guns grapeshot!" shouted Ash.

The Navy's gun crews responded fast, lowering the elevation so the cannons were now sighting directly at the gunports of the pirate vessel. When each cannon maw pointed at the target, the lead gunner roared, "On!" to notify the commander they were ready to fire.

The order came moments later.

The cannons fired a storm of grapeshot, ripping life from their enemy. The enemy gunners did not scream, they did not complain. They couldn't. All but a few of them lay dead, bright red blood, chunks of brain or slithers of entrails sliding between the gaps in the floorboards.

The grappling hooks hauled the ships close together, forming one massive flotilla and ensuring the pirate vessel—tricked into combat against what they assumed was a weak opponent—couldn't flee.

Ash's eyes narrowed as he focused upon the Marine standing

at the front of the throng. *Who is that?* He smiled as realisation dawned. *Corporal Dane. Damn good soldier, a good choice to lead them across into the enemy.*

"Send in the Marines!" Ash shouted.

Corporal Dane, kneeling by the ship's gunwale, checked the leather stock wrapped around his neck, tugging on it to ensure it was firmly fixed in place. The thick leather would protect the flesh of his throat from a knife or a glancing blow from a bayonet or bullet. There was a legend that the leather stock of one Royal Marine had stopped a musket round but Dane had always doubted it. He inspected the bayonet affixed to the end of his musket and ensured it wasn't loose. Satisfied, he cast a look at the flash pan of his weapon to ensure it was prepared correctly, the hammer fully cocked. His index finger was placed safely outside the trigger guard, resting on the wooden stock, pointing towards the barrel. He looked over his shoulder at those who knelt nearby. "You boot necks ready?"

A young lad by the name of Yams, leather stock similarly wrapped around his neck, grinned, flashing yellowed teeth. "Let's áve the bastards!"

"Gibraltar!" roared Lieutenant Marks — the code word for the

Marines to board the enemy vessel.

Dane looked up at the Marines nestled in the rigging high above him. The closest one, Nock Gun pulled into his shoulder, glared back. Dane nodded and rose into a half-crouch, motioning with one hand at the Marines behind to prepare to move.

BOOM! The Nock Guns roared their deafening fury down upon the enemy deck, rounds of lead slamming into soft flesh or lodging in bone. Dane was up, one boot on the gunwale, musket brought back so the buttstock was under his armpit. He launched himself across onto the pirate ship, leading with cold, sharp steel.

A man, face covered in grime, held a dirty cutlass in front of him.

He brought the weapon over his shoulder to better strike at the first Royal Marine to arrive. Dane's boots hit the gunwale of the enemy ship, and he shoved his musket forward, allowing momentum to carry the bayonet deep into Grim Face's chest, long before the man could bring his cutlass down. He ripped the bayonet clear and shoulder barged a man out of the way. Dane lunged at another pirate, the bayonet sliding into his belly up to the musket's barrel. The man collapsed to the deck, holding his guts in the foetal position. A loud crack nearby sent a round buzzing past his nose. Dane swore and kicked the knee out from under the tall, skinny, pistol-wielding man and broke clear of the enemy's ranks.

Running into the middle of the deck, he turned to watch the progress of the Royal Marines who'd followed him. "On me!" he yelled.

Four made it through the gap behind him and sprinted towards him. The others were fighting hand-to-hand against the enemy. They had linked up so that a small ball of blue coats stayed together against the onslaught of pirates.

"Line facing that direction!" Dane shouted at the Marines with him, ensuring they'd be firing at the pirates farthest from his Marines, battling their way toward him.

They formed a line, shoulder to shoulder.

"Present!"

Weapons were pulled into

shoulders, determined faces staring down gun sights. The discharge of Dane's weapon would be the command to fire. He nestled the weapon's sights on a lanky man charging over. Other pirates noticed the tiny formation of Marines nearby and made a beeline towards them. Dane swore again.

He squeezed the trigger and the weapon bucked into his shoulder, the roar blasting all other noise clear of his head, and the pirate disappeared behind a cloud of gun smoke. High-pitched whistling filled his ears. The smoke cleared fast, and Dane's target was down, blood spilled out onto the deck from the hole in his throat. Another two pirates were down, one dead and the other writhing on the ground, clutching his stomach. There'd be no time to reload before the remaining prates were on them.

"Stand fast!" Dane roared, bringing his musket back so the buttstock was in his armpit. The Marines on either side of him remained where they stood, their sharp bayonets at the ready, polished metal glinting on the tips.

The pirate leading the charge sported an unkempt beard through which he shrieked some unintelligible sound. His broad-brimmed hat was stained with what looked suspiciously like mud or faecal matter. Dane was painfully aware there wasn't much mud around on the open seas. The pirate held a cutlass high above his head, preparing to bring it down in an overhead cut. He was fast, much faster than his comrades. A good thing if it were a foot race. But it wasn't.

"Let's have ya!" Dane shouted. The Marine took two short steps forward and rammed his musket forward hard, the bayonet punched into the pirate's chest. Through the wooden stock, Dane felt the grind of cold steel cutting along the edge of ribs. The pirate's face, once lined with fury and confidence, morphed to agony and disbelief. Dane kicked the man from the end of his weapon and stepped back into line with his Marines.

Then the larger group of pirates arrived, some armed with

pistols, others with knives, a few with muskets, and one with a small wooden club. The Marines held a tiny defensive position bristling with sharp steel.

"ON GUARD!" The Marines roared and met the onslaught with their bayonets.

Dane slammed his bayonet into a man's throat, withdrew it, parried a sword then buried sharp steel into the guts of his assailant. A pirate pushed the mortally wounded man aside and stopped, a bayonet in his chest. Dane twisted the weapon and pulled the blade free, then blocked an attack from the club-wielding savage. The attack was powerful, the blow almost dislodging the musket from Dane's grasp. He recovered and lunged, putting a hole in the man's stomach.

With the pirates' attention turned towards the tiny group of Marines, they neglected to consider the majority behind them. The blue coats advanced, attacking from behind and overwhelming them within minutes. The survivors sprinted away, fear and terror fuelling their speed.

"Form two ranks!" yelled Dane.

The Marines obliged.

"Front rank, kneel!"

Dane was aware the majority of Marines had not yet discharged their weapons.

"Present!" Weapons were pulled into their shoulders. "FIRE!"

Muskets roared, casting

clouds of acrid gunpowder across the deck. When the pall cleared, the remaining pirates were down, some still moving and groaning. One was attempting to crawl away, a trail of blood smearing the deck behind him.

"Reload!"

The Marines were fast, able to reload a musket in fifteen seconds.

"Present! Fire!"

Another deafening staccato of musket fire ripped the sky asunder. Pirates lay in lifeless disarray.

"Front rank stand! Advance!"

The front rank of Marines, leading with their bayonets, walked towards the pile of bodies.

"Kill any pirate who lives!"

Captain Ash stood ramrod straight, hands clasped behind his back and watched his Royal Marines board the enemy ship. The pirates stood little chance. They might have the numbers but they lacked the discipline, skill, and sheer ferocity of the Marines. Their ship had been irreparably damaged, and they'd already suffered casualties before the engagement, so the odds had already been stacked against them. The pricey cost of being lured in by deception. Maybe ten minutes after the hand-to-hand skirmish started, it was over, the pirates having suffered a resounding and merciless defeat.

Ash turned to the nearby Lieutenant Basby, who'd been watching the fight as well. "XO! You have the helm!"

"Aye, sir."

Captain Ash descended the short flight of stars onto the deck proper and strode towards a gangplank that bridged the two ships. A sailor stood at attention and saluted as he approached. Ash snapped a return salute. "Stand easy," he muttered.

In two steps, he jumped down onto the deck of the pirate ship and immediately felt it listing slightly to port, suggesting one or several cannon shots had punctured the planks beneath the ocean's surface, allowing water to gush into the hold. *Another hour or two and she'll be on the bottom.* A slight smile teased the corners of his mouth. *Good!* The bodies of dead pirates lay strewn across the deck, the acrid aroma of blood and shit tainting the air, even overwhelming the scent of the sea. A couple of Marines stood nearby. One held his musket so the buttstock of the weapon rested upon the wooden floor, bayonet pointing at the sky. The other wound a bandage around the forearm of a comrade.

Ash approached them. "He'll live, I trust?"

The Marines glanced up. "Aye, sir," the injured man replied. "Just got clumsy is all."

As far as Ash could tell, he was the only injured Marine. He nodded. "Good work, men!" Then he walked towards the helm of the enemy ship. Jogging up the stairs, he made it to the wheel in front of which knelt the pirate captain and another man. Around them stood Royal Marines, muskets pointed at the kneeling men. Nearby lay a few corpses, the face of one disfigured as a result of a musket ball drilling a hole through where his nose had once been.

Captain Ash stopped in front of the pair and glared. "It seems your men were more accustomed to fighting women and children than His Majesty's Royal Marines." Ash chuckled, and gestured to the small group of corpses nearby. "They didn't account for themselves very well." The enemy captain glared up at him. "None of you did."

The pirate beside the enemy captain leaned forward and spat on Ash's boot. In less time than it took to blink, Ash had his pistol clear from its holster and levelled at the face of the pirate.

The man's eyes grew wide, and raised his hands in either surrender or to seek mercy.

Ash pulled the trigger.

The pistol bucked in his hand with a loud retort, barrel spewing a cloud of burnt powder. The round cut a hole through the left eye of the kneeling man, blowing out the back of his head. His body crashed onto the deck, blood leaking onto the already stained wood around him.

The kneeling captain, the right side of his face now splattered with blood and tiny chunks of brain, inhaled sharply through his teeth.

"I have a few questions for you," Ash continued in a conversational tone as he wiped his spit-covered boot onto the corpse at his feet. "First, what's your name?"

"Captain Rourke," the man gritted out.

Ash laughed, a hearty sound which made a few of the Marines grin. "My dear man, you are no captain." He opened a pouch by his side, and brought out a small packet. Ripping it open at one corner with his teeth, he spat the sliver of paper onto the ground then poured black powder down the muzzle of the pistol. "I will just call you Rourke."

Rourke's wide eyes remained on the pistol, watching Ash reload.

"How many pirate ships are off the east coast of England?"

The pirate's eyes darted between the pistol and Ash's face. "I'm not sure. I think there might be somewhere around three or four."

A smile teased Ash's mouth. He dropped a round down the muzzle of the pistol. "'Somewhere around' isn't very precise. I need an exact number." He shoved the now-empty paper packet down the pistol's muzzle and withdrew the small ramrod from beneath the barrel.

Rourke watched, transfixed and terrified. "Seven." His dry

tongue flicked out between dry lips and then disappeared again. "Seven between here and York."

Ash nodded. He tamped down the satchel, ball, and powder. "That's more like it. Seven, you say? What size are they?" His thumb pulled back the flintlock hammer, and finally, his eyes came to rest upon Rourke.

The pirate noticed that Ash did not re-holster the weapon. "None smaller than forty guns." Rourke stared at the pistol, eyes like dinner plates. "Please don't kill me, I beg you!"

Ash's eyebrows drew together, and he pursed his lips. "Explain to me why I should not?"

"Because I'm unarmed!"

Ash nodded. "As were the

villagers you raided. Yet you still killed them. I remain unconvinced. Try again."

"My life as a pirate is ended. I'll never hurt another innocent person, I swear it!"

Ash nodded slowly. "I will let you live as I feel particularly merciful today. But I have a task for you, Rourke."

"Anything!"

"Before you give up on your life of piracy, I want you to spread the word to the other pirates out there that Captain Ash is coming for them. Tell them I'll send them to the bottom of the ocean and their souls to hell." Ash holstered his pistol. "And Rourke?"

The kneeling man stared at Ash, a wet patch spreading across his trousers at his groin. "If I catch you fighting on one of those pirate ships, the best you could ever pray for is a round through the skull. I'll make your death slow and painful beyond your worst nightmares."

"You have my word."

Ash snorted. "Your word is worth less than your shit-stained existence. But I believe you." He turned to the Marines nearby. "Give him the rowboat as well as rations and water."

"Aye, sir," the closest said. "How many days of rations, sir?"

"Days? No. Give him enough rations and water for half a day." He looked at Rourke. "See? We are not complete barbarians." Ash's smile was hardened steel. "Spread the word amongst your pirate compatriots,   Rourke.   Death approaches. Now get your arse off this ship!"

1779, London

Silence filled the room, although the occasional distant clopping and rattle of a horse-drawn cart drifted in from the half-open window. Rear Admiral James Roy leaned back in his chair, a wooden squeak breaking the stillness of the room. Roy stroked his chin, eyes darting across the words on the parchment in his hand. When he'd finished reading, he placed the parchment upon the polished surface of the table and smiled. "The pirates have met their match."

If you liked this, you'll like Keith's other books:

www.ingramcontent.com/pod-product-compliance
Lightning Source LLC
Chambersburg PA
CBHW010320100726
47906CB00006B/1066